HAWKEYE COLLINS & AMY ADAMS in

THE SECRET OF THE
SOFTWARE
SPY & 8 OTHER MYSTERIES

by M. MASTERS

Spotlight reinforced library bound edition copyright © 2007. Spotlight is a division of ABDO Publishing Company, Edina, Minnesota.

Copyright © 1983 by Meadowbrook Creations

All stories written by Alexander von Wacker
Illustrations by Brett Gadbois
Editor: Kathe Grooms
Assistant Editor: Louise Delagran
Design: Terry Dugan
Production: John Ware, Donna Ahrens
Cover Art: Robert Sauber

ISBN-10 1-59961-147-3 (reinforced library bound edition)
ISBN-13 978-1-59961-147-1 (reinforced library bound edition)

Library of Congress Cataloging-In-Publication Data

This title was previously cataloged with the following information:

Masters, M.
    Hawkeye Collins & Amy Adams in The secret of the software spy & 8 other mysteries.
    (Can you solve the mystery?TM ; #8)
    Summary: Hawkeye Collins and Amy Adams, two twelve-year-old sleuths, solve nine mysteries using Hawkeye's sketches of important clues. The reader is asked to use Hawkeye's sketches and hints to solve the mysteries.
    [1. Mystery and detective stories. 2. Literary recreations.] I. Title. II. Title: Hawkeye Collins and Amy Adams in The secret of the software spy & 8 other mysteries. III. Title: Secret of the software spy. IV. Series: Masters, M. Can you solve the mystery?™
PZ7.M42392Hl   1983   [Fic]   83-17319

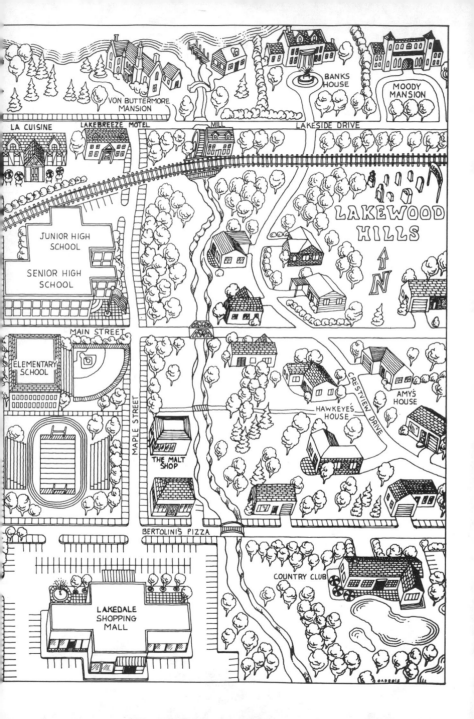

Dear Readers,

You can solve these mysteries along with us! Start by reading very carefully -- Watch out for things like what people <u>say</u> happened, the ways they behave, and details like the time and the weather. Then look closely at the sketch or other picture clue with the story. If you remember the facts, the picture clue should help you break the case.

If you want to check your answer -- or if a hard case stumps you -- turn to the solutions at the back of the book. They're written in mirror type. Hold them up to a mirror and they'll look right. If you don't have a mirror, turn the page and hold it up to the light. (You can teach yourself to read backwards, too. We can do it pretty well now and it comes in handy some times in our cases.)

Have fun -- we sure did!

Amy

Hawkeye

The Mystery of the Missing Turkey

Hawkeye Collins and Amy Adams, the twelve-year-old super sleuths of Lakewood Hills, were hot on the trail of another exciting mystery.

"Where's the electric mixer?" shouted Hawkeye.

It was Thanksgiving. The Collins and Adams families, along with Sergeant Treadwell, the local policeman, and his wife, were all in the kitchen preparing dinner.

Hawkeye's father, a lawyer, was making a sauce for the vegetables. Mrs. Collins was hauling dishes out of a cabinet and carrying them into the dining room, where she had just cleared away some papers from her real-estate business. Amy's

1

parents were hovering over the turkey, trying to decide if it was done.

Amy pulled out a chair and stood on it. "Has anyone seen the electric mixer?" she repeated impatiently. "Hawkeye and I are in charge of the pies, and no electric mixer means no whipped cream!"

Sergeant Treadwell patted his pudgy stomach. "What's Thanksgiving without whipped cream?" he asked.

Mr. Collins looked up. "If you two can't find the mixer, it's probably not in the house."

"Oh, brother," said Amy, rolling her green eyes. " 'The Mystery of the Missing Electric Mixer.' Now, there's a hot case."

"Hey, where's Lucy?" said Hawkeye, scratching his blond hair and looking around for Amy's six-year-old sister.

"I don't know," Amy answered. "She's supposed to be in charge of the mashed potatoes."

Just then, Hawkeye heard a low hum coming from the back of the house.

He quickly scanned the kitchen counters, his sharp eyes rapidly taking in everything. Everything, that is, but any trace of mashed potatoes.

He turned to Amy. "Lucy's got the mixer! And I bet that's her in the back of the house."

They raced each other out of the room. Amy, star of the track team, ran ahead. The humming noise was coming from the bathroom, and

they came to a halt outside the door.

Amy cleared her throat. "Oh, Lucy?" she called sweetly. "Yoo-hoo, Lucy? Are you in there?"

The noise stopped. It was a moment before Lucy, who was missing her front teeth, spoke.

"What i*th* it?" replied Lucy, "I'm b*ithy*!"

Amy glanced at Hawkeye and groaned, but continued speaking pleasantly.

"Lucy, what are you doing in there?"

"You haven't seen the electric mixer, have you, Luce?" added Hawkeye.

Lucy snapped, "I'm blow-drying my hair! Now leave me alone!"

"Lucy," began Amy, a little impatiently, "are you mashing the potatoes in there?"

Lucy flung open the door. She stood on a stool, electric mixer in hand. A large glass bowl of semi-mashed potatoes sat on the counter next to the toothbrushes.

"Well, what if I am?" demanded Lucy, pointing the mixer toward Hawkeye and Amy. "The kitchen wa*th* too crowded. And I want to do a real good job on the*the* potatoe*th*!"

Suddenly the hall phone began to ring. At the same moment, a big blob of mashed potatoes fell from the mixer and plopped onto the bathroom floor.

"Oop*th*!" said Lucy. "Hawkeye, where'*th* your dog? She'll lick it up."

"Lucy!" shouted Amy. "That's gross!"

3

The phone kept ringing. As Hawkeye walked down the hall to answer it, he also tried to figure out where his golden retriever, Nosey, was.

"Hey, come to think of it, I don't know where she is," he said, reaching for the phone. "In fact, I haven't seen her all morning."

Hawkeye picked up the receiver on the fifth ring. "Hello?" he said.

A mean, scratchy voice screamed, "Your dog stole my turkey!"

"Mrs. Ratchet?" he said hesitantly. All the kids in the neighborhood knew that Mrs. Ratchet was the meanest person in town.

"Yes, you fool, I'm Mrs. Ratchet! And yes, your dog stole my turkey!"

Hawkeye gulped. "Nosey wouldn't do a thing like that. She—she wouldn't steal anyone's turkey."

"She's not home now, is she?" Mrs. Ratchet replied in a cranky voice.

"Well, actually, I'm not sure—"

"See! It *was* your dog!" Mrs. Ratchet exclaimed. "I saw her outside an hour ago. Then I put my turkey on my back porch to cool a bit. When I came back, it was gone."

Mrs. Ratchet paused to catch her breath, then really screamed. "Just you wait 'til I catch that dog!"

Hawkeye held the phone away from his ear as Mrs. Ratchet blasted away. When she was

through, he spoke quickly.

"I'll be right over, okay? 'Bye."

Hawkeye hung up the phone and turned to Amy.

"Forget the whipped cream and the mashed potatoes!" he said. "Nosey's in big trouble and we have to save her before Mrs. Ratchet catches her!"

Leaving Lucy in the bathroom with the potatoes, Hawkeye and Amy hurried out of the house and hopped on their ten-speeds.

A half-hour later, they rode past Von Buttermore Park, then turned into Mrs. Ratchet's driveway. She was standing in the middle of the pavement, a scowl on her face and a broom in her hand.

"It was your dog who stole my turkey!" she yelled. "I saw that dog—the one with the big nose—out here sniffing around less than an hour before I put my turkey out to cool."

Hawkeye glanced about quickly. "But have you seen her since? Have you seen Nosey at all?"

"No!" hollered Mrs. Ratchet. "And I haven't seen my turkey, either!"

Amy said, "But if you didn't actually see Nosey taking the turkey, how do you know for sure that she did it? Maybe someone else came along and stole it."

Mrs. Ratchet pointed to the back yard with her broom.

"I have proof," she said. "I'll show you."

Hawkeye and Amy paused for a minute before following Mrs. Ratchet. "I'm not sure I want to see this," Hawkeye whispered to Amy.

"Do you really think Nosey ate her turkey?" Amy asked him.

"I don't know," Hawkeye replied. "But if she did, she's probably going to be one real sick dog."

They started after Mrs. Ratchet.

"Has Nosey ever done anything like this before?" asked Amy.

"Well, last year she ate all the candy canes off the Christmas tree." Hawkeye shook his head. "Boy, was she sick—all over Mom's present to Dad."

"Oh, gross," Amy muttered.

From up ahead, Mrs. Ratchet yelled, "What are you kids dawdling for? Come here! Come here, I say!" With her broom, she pointed to something on the ground. "Here's your proof."

Hawkeye and Amy hurried forward. On the ground, just a few feet from the back steps, was a foil roasting pan. Except for a bit of juice and some stuffing on the bottom, it was empty.

"See?" said Mrs. Ratchet. "Look at those teeth marks. That's how I know it was your dog. That foul creature must have dragged the pan off the porch, then picked up the turkey and run off."

Amy was doubtful. "But how could a dog pick up a turkey and carry it away? Don't most turkeys weigh a lot—like fifteen or twenty pounds?"

Mrs. Ratchet pulled her broom close against her body.

"That's a turkey for a family," she said curtly. "But my turkey was just for me, so it wasn't large."

Hawkeye stared at her.

"You mean, you were going to have Thanksgiving dinner alone?"

"Of course!" Mrs. Ratchet snapped defensively.

Suddenly Amy's green eyes widened.

"Look, there's Nosey!"

Hawkeye's dog was trotting across the back yard toward them. Carrying a frisbee in her mouth, Nosey looked as happy as could be.

"She's feasted on my turkey, and now she wants to play!" Mrs. Ratchet exclaimed angrily, raising her broom and charging toward the dog. "I'll show her!"

Amy burst into a run and cut Mrs. Ratchet off before she could reach Nosey.

"No, Mrs. Ratchet, don't hit her!" said Amy.

"She's just a dog!" said Hawkeye, rushing forward.

Mrs. Ratchet stopped. She put her hands on her hips and scowled at Hawkeye and Amy.

"Just a dog, is she?" she said nastily. "Well, I'm calling the dog pound right now and I'm going to insist that they lock that mongrel up!"

Broom in hand, Mrs. Ratchet turned and

stormed into the house. Hawkeye and Amy looked at one another, then at Nosey.

"Did you really steal that turkey?" Hawkeye asked Nosey.

"Maybe you should smell her breath," suggested Amy.

"Hawkeye turned to her. "*You* smell it."

"No way," said Amy, backing away.

Sensing something was wrong, Nosey crept up to Hawkeye with her ears laid back. She looked up at him sheepishly. Then she dropped the frisbee at his feet, beside the empty roasting pan.

"Nosey, this is not a time to play!" Hawkeye said, frowning at his dog. "You might be on your way to prison."

Hawkeye automatically pulled out his sketch pad and pencil. He was an excellent artist, quick and accurate. Sketching the scene of the crime helped him solve mysteries.

"If Nosey's innocent," said Hawkeye to Amy, "I've got to save her by finding a clue that will prove it!"

Amy didn't look very hopeful. "Well, we'd better hurry. Mrs. Ratchet's going to be right back."

Hawkeye sketched as fast as he could. His hand moved up and down, carefully drawing everything he saw. Moments later, he was finished.

Holding the drawing out to Amy, he said, "I don't see anything."

"If Nosey's innocent," said Hawkeye, "I've got to find a clue that will prove it!"

Amy studied the drawing.

The next instant, Mrs. Ratchet came flying out of the house.

"The dog catcher's on his way over," she yelled.

Just then, Hawkeye spotted the clue he had been searching for.

"Wait a minute, Mrs. Ratchet!" he said, pointing to his drawing. "Nosey didn't steal your turkey—and I can prove it!"

HOW DID HAWKEYE KNOW THAT NOSEY HADN'T STOLEN MRS. RATCHET'S TURKEY?

SOLUTION

See page 69

The Case of the Tinsel-Teeth Teaser

Hawkeye sighed dramatically as he and Amy came out of biology class.

"Maybe I should be a surgeon," he joked.

"Oh, come on," said Amy, short on patience. "People are a lot different than frogs, you know. Just because you did the best dissection in class doesn't mean you're ready to operate on people."

As they rounded a corner, they smashed right into Joanna Simpson, a girl in their class.

"Leave me alone!" she snapped as she wiped her eyes with one arm.

"Hey, cool it. We didn't see you," said Amy. Noticing that the girl's eyes were all wet, Amy asked, "Is something the matter?"

11

"Yeah, what happened?" said Hawkeye.

Joanna wiped her eyes and raised her head. As she spoke, she covered her mouth with her hand.

"Oh, am I glad it's you guys," Joanna said, sniffling.

Hawkeye asked, "What's up? Are you in some kind of trouble?"

"I'll say."

Joanna glanced to either side, and when she was sure no one except Hawkeye and Amy could see, she uncovered her mouth. In an instant she flashed them a little, sad smile that was bulging with braces.

She sighed. "In case you hadn't noticed, I just got braces. And someone's been sending me these really creepy letters ever since. I just got another one. Do you think you could help me find out who's sending them? Then maybe I could make them stop."

"Sure," said Hawkeye. "Do you have the letter? Let me see it."

Joanna dried her eyes. "It's in my locker right down there. I'll get it."

Amy glanced up at the hall clock. "Sorry, but I can't help right now. I'm already late for track practice. But don't worry. Hawkeye's as good at dissecting mysteries as he is at cutting up frogs."

"Oh, ish," said Joanna as she turned down the hall toward her locker.

Hawkeye groaned. "Bag it, Amy!"

Giggling to herself, Amy trotted off down the hall.

Joanna returned, holding the note out for Hawkeye to read.

"Here you are, Hawkeye," said Joanna.

Hawkeye took the note and turned it over in his hand before reading it. "Was the paper wrinkled like this when you got it?" he asked.

"No, I kind of smashed it all up after I read it," said Joanna. "I was so angry. Someone slid it into my locker. That's where I found it."

"What strange writing," said Hawkeye, as he took the note. It was written with a broad, felt-tip pen and the handwriting which was fairly neat, slanted sharply to the left.

Hey, Tinsel Teeth!

What a beautiful mouth you have! I mean, it looks ridiculous to the max. Your ugly smile is now so bright that hardly anyone can stand to look at you. Hope you meet the tin man of your dreams!

The Tooth Fairy

"What a creep!" Hawkeye handed it back to her. "Do you know who might have written it?"

Joanna thought for a moment. She hesitated.

13

"Well, I think it's one of the girls in this group that's always making fun of me. My mother says it's because they're jealous I'm a cheerleader," she explained.

"Did you ask them about the notes?" Hawkeye asked.

"No, 'cause they'd never admit it," Joanna replied. "But if I could prove it, then I could talk to them and make 'em stop."

Hawkeye nodded. "Do you know where these girls are now?"

"Yes, the library," Joanna said.

"Let me put my books in my locker. Then you can point them out to me," Hawkeye said.

"Well, okay," said Joanna, a bit reluctantly, "but don't say anything to them, okay?"

A few minutes later they entered the large library, which was filled with groups of students studying. Moving cautiously, they cut behind the book shelves. Suddenly Joanna stopped. She peered through the stacks.

"There," she whispered. "That's them. It's that group of girls."

By bending over and looking through the books, Hawkeye could make out a group of six girls sitting at a table. All of them were studying.

Hawkeye turned to Joanna and said quietly, "I'm going to do a quick drawing. Wait for me out in the hall. If they spot you they'll be suspicious."

"I know who's been writing you those notes," said Hawkeye.

"You're right," agreed Joanna quickly.

Hawkeye pretended to be writing a list of book titles, but instead did a complete drawing of the six girls sitting at the table. Peering over and around the books, he tried to include as much detail as he could.

Minutes later he was finished with the drawing. He examined it, a slight frown on his face, and then it struck him.

"Of course!" he said to himself.

Drawing in hand, he hurried into the hall, where Joanna was patiently waiting.

"Did you find anything?" she asked.

"You bet," said Hawkeye, handing her the drawing and the note. "I know who's been writing you those notes."

WHO WROTE THE NOTE TO JOANNA?

See page 73

The Case of the China Catastrophe

"Hey, how do you like my new, improved hot fudge sundae?" asked Sergeant Treadwell, the pudgiest policeman in Lakewood Hills. "I think the colored sprinkles kind of brighten it up."

Hawkeye studied his heaping sundae and said, "Sprinkles are awesome, Sarge. No doubt about it."

Amy nodded. "For sure."

Hot fudge sundaes were not only Sergeant Treadwell's specialty, they were also his way of thanking Hawkeye and Amy for their help on difficult cases. They had just helped Sarge find out who had thrown toilet paper all over Mrs. Ratchet's trees.

Just then the phone rang. Sergeant Treadwell, who had just taken an enormous bite of ice cream, slapped his hand over his mouth and tried to speak.

"Era ibildiido!"

"What?" said Amy laughing.

"Era ibildiido!"

Hawkeye couldn't help laughing, too. "I think he wants one of us to answer the phone."

Hawkeye cleared his throat and reached for the phone. He deepened his voice as much as he could.

"Police station, Sergeant Treadwell's office!"

A man's voice at the other end yelled, "This is Mark Norton from The China Closet. Someone just smashed half of the china in my store!"

Hawkeye held the phone away from his ear. The man was yelling so loudly that both Amy and Sergeant Treadwell could hear.

"We'll be right there!" said Hawkeye in his regular voice.

Amy put her sundae down and put her sweater on, buttoning it right over left. "Well, there's always a mystery in Lakewood Hills."

The sergeant reluctantly put their sundaes in the little fridge under the table. The three of them hurried out of the police station and into the warm afternoon air. They ran past the Civil War cannon, and reached The China Closet mo-

ments later. Amy, the fastest of the bunch, was there first, Hawkeye right behind her. Huffing and puffing, Sergeant Treadwell arrived seconds later.

"Wow!" said Amy, going in.

Hawkeye's mouth fell open. "Wow, this is even worse than when Nosey ran through the garage sale and knocked down all those old plates and cups!"

Broken china and glass were everywhere. An enormous shelf was tipped over, and shattered plates were scattered all across the floor. Hawkeye spotted Mr. Norton standing at the rear of the store.

"This is awful, Mr. Norton." Hawkeye grabbed his sketch pad from his back pocket. "What happened? You aren't hurt, are you?"

Breathless, Sergeant Treadwell came in. "Holy sundaes! What the heck happened?"

Mr. Norton shook his head in disbelief. "Pretty bad, huh? Me, I'm—I'm fine. But look at this mess!"

"Well, were you robbed or something?" asked Amy, trying to get some information.

"That's just it." Mr. Norton tried to take a few steps forward. "I don't know what happened. I had been unpacking some new china out here, and then I went in the back room to check the rest of the order. Suddenly there was this enormous crash. I came running out here and this whole shelf full of my best china and crystal was

smashed all over the floor!"

"Did it fall or did someone tip it over?" asked Hawkeye.

"Someone tipped it." Mr. Norton walked across the shop, wincing as pieces of china crunched beneath his feet. "I don't know who because I was in the back room, but I heard someone come in the front door. I was just about to come out front when I heard the crash. Whoever it was had already run away by the time I got out here."

Hawkeye and Amy tried to clear some of the broken dishes so they could move around and look for clues. They picked up the larger pieces and stacked them to the side.

"Now, don't you worry," said the sergeant, pulling out his report book. "We'll get to the bottom of this and, um, somehow we'll find out who—"

"Hey, look at that!" said Amy.

Amy unhooked a sweater that was caught by some threads on a hook near the door. She held it up for everyone to see.

"It's a letter sweater from Lakewood High!" said Hawkeye.

"It sure is," said Amy, nodding. She noticed a small pin attached to it. "And look, it's from the basketball team."

Sergeant Treadwell turned to Mr. Norton. "Was this here before? Could it belong to whoever did this?"

"I'll bet it does," said Mr. Norton. "I just cleaned up before I went in the back. I'm sure it wasn't here."

Amy noticed something on the sweater. She bent over and squinted.

"Hey, there are a couple of red hairs on here!" she said.

Sergeant Treadwell snapped his fingers.

"Say, now," he said, "I've been to a few of the basketball games over at Lakewood High. There're a couple of guys on the team with red hair. I'll call the coach and get their names."

Sergeant Treadwell clumsily made his way through the mess to the phone. As the sergeant began dialing, Hawkeye turned to Amy.

"I'll bet we can find some other clues on the sweater," said Hawkeye, opening his pad to a clean page.

"Right," said Amy, laying the sweater on a pile of dishes. "I'll check the pockets while you draw."

Hawkeye studied the sweater, shifting his eyes from it to his pad. His first few lines were general, the rest more precise.

Amy fished around in the pocket. "Hey, there's some money here!" she said, pulling out a crumpled five-dollar bill. "And there's a house key and an empty potato-chip bag in the other pocket."

"Good, good!"

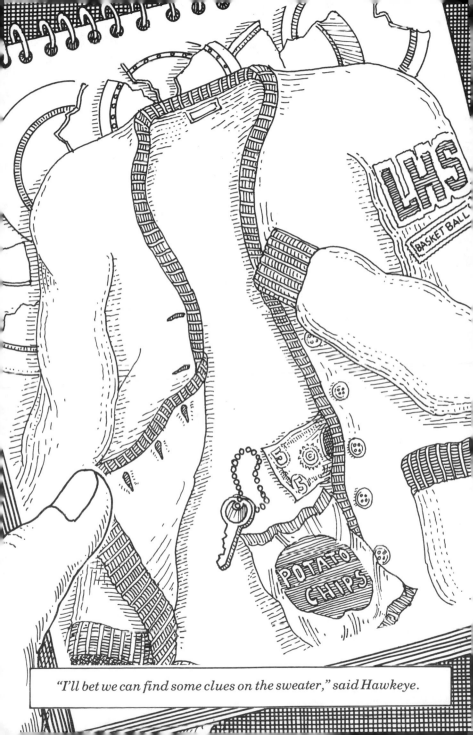

"I'll bet we can find some clues on the sweater," said Hawkeye.

Hawkeye drew quickly, and was careful to include all the things Amy had found. But when he was finished a few minutes later, he wasn't sure what to make of it.

"Take a look at this, Amy." He held out the drawing. "There's a lot of stuff here, but I'm not sure what it means."

Amy stepped over a few broken wine glasses and looked at Hawkeye's drawing. Seconds later, she gasped.

"Of course!" she said, slapping her forehead. "Why didn't I see that earlier? Hawkeye, we're sort of on the wrong track. But now I know where we should start looking!"

WHERE SHOULD THEY LOOK FOR THE CULPRIT WHO SMASHED ALL THE CHINA?

See page 75

The Secret of the Mysterious Letters

"Help!" cried a grey-haired woman. "Help!"

Hawkeye and Amy were in downtown Minneapolis. They had just hopped off the red city bus from Lakewood Hills.

"Did you hear that?" asked Hawkeye.

Quickly turning her head from side to side, Amy said, "Yeah, but where—?"

"Help!" cried the voice again. "That woman stole my briefcase!"

Hawkeye and Amy, who were on their way to a Twins baseball game at the Metrodome, ran over to the woman who had been shouting for help.

"What happened?" asked Hawkeye.

"Are you all right?" said Amy.

"I'm fine, but that woman over there stole my briefcase! I must get it back—I have some important legal documents in it!"

The grey-haired lady pointed down the street toward a young blond woman. The woman, who was wearing a dark-blue coat and running as fast as she could, had the stolen briefcase in one hand and some books in the other.

"Right there! That's her!" cried the old woman. "Stop her—she has my briefcase!"

Amy automatically burst into a run. "We'll catch her!"

Hawkeye took off at the same instant. "Stop that thief!" he shouted.

Up ahead, the woman in the dark-blue coat cut through a crowd of people. She shoved aside a man in a business suit, then hurried around a corner.

"We've got to catch her!" shouted Amy, running as fast as she could.

Without replying, Hawkeye zoomed around a group of people on their lunch break. By the time they reached the corner, the blond woman was nowhere to be seen.

"Wait, there she is!" said Hawkeye, pointing to the entrance of a tall building.

The blond thief glanced around without slowing down. Just then, she smashed right into a large man. The stolen briefcase and the books went flying.

"She dropped the case!" shouted Hawkeye. "Now's our chance!"

"Stop that woman!" yelled Amy. "She stole that briefcase!"

But the blond woman quickly scooped up the stolen goods and ran off. She hurried into the office building and in a moment was out of sight.

When they reached the spot where the woman had dropped the briefcase, Amy exclaimed, "We lost her!"

Hawkeye came to a halt and looked around desperately. The thief had vanished.

Then he spotted something on the sidewalk. "Hey, there's one of the books she dropped!"

Amy bent over and picked it up. "I hope this has some kind of clue for us—we need one." She thumbed through the book. "Hmm, doesn't look like it."

Suddenly, three envelopes fell to the ground from the back of the book.

"Look!" said Hawkeye, reaching for the envelopes. "These might give us our clue."

All three of the white envelopes had addresses written neatly on them. Hawkeye and Amy flipped through them.

"Look at the addresses," Amy said. "I bet we could find out who the thief is if we contact these people."

"No, wait—maybe we don't even have to

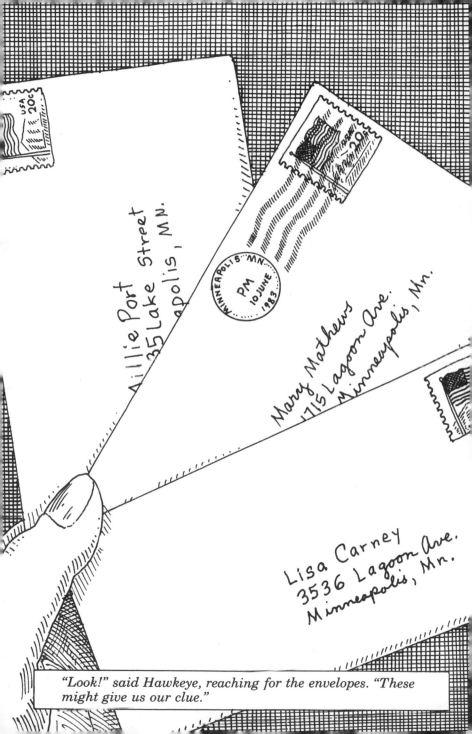

"Look!" said Hawkeye, reaching for the envelopes. "These might give us our clue."

do that." Hawkeye scratched his head in puzzlement. "There's something here, but— but I'm not sure what."

"Listen, Hawkeye," said Amy, handing him the book. "I'm going to go find the woman whose briefcase was stolen. I'll be right back."

Hawkeye, lost in thought, nodded. "Right."

Hawkeye made his way over to a bench and sat down. He spread the three envelopes out side by side, then tapped his head with his finger.

"Logic," he muttered. "This one's just pure logic."

He sat there thinking until Amy returned a couple of minutes later. Right behind her was the grey-haired woman.

Suddenly, the answer came to him.

"Come on!" he said, leaping to his feet. "We have to tell the police who stole the briefcase!"

A hopeful smile appeared on the woman's face. "You mean, you know who she was?"

"Yes, ma'am," said Hawkeye, holding up the envelopes. "Her name's right here!"

"Good work, Hawkeye!" Amy exclaimed, grinning. "We might be able to make the start of the ball game, after all!"

WHO STOLE THE GREY-HAIRED WOMAN'S BRIEFCASE?

See page 79

The Mystery of Molly's Phone Call

"What was your best dare ever?" asked Hawkeye, as he sat at Pronto Pizza with Justin and Amy.

"Well—" Justin, who could never turn down a dare, thought awhile. "That's a tough question. But just last week, my brother dared me to call the bank and try to goof up the computer."

"How can you do that with a bank's computer?" asked Amy, laughing.

"Well, you know, a touch-tone phone is the only way you can communicate with a computer over the telephone lines. So anyway, he dared me

31

to call, and then, instead of punching in my account number, to play 'Yankee Doodle' over the phone. But—"

Justin's words were cut off by Paul Townsend, the young manager of Pronto Pizza, and the only one in the kitchen that day.

"Molly!" he yelled at his younger sister. "Get off that phone! You know you can't make long-distance phone calls from here."

The young man stormed out from behind the counter and over to the phone. Without saying another word, he yanked the receiver out of his sister's hand and hung it up.

"Omigosh, like I'm totally bummed," whined Molly in a high voice. She was sitting on a chair beneath the wall phone. "Like, I know you're my brother, Paul, okay? But you can, like, really be a jerk to the max. Like, a total geek, you know? Like, I'm really edged, fer sure!"

"In here, I'm not your brother," replied Paul. "In here, I'm the manager of Pronto Pizza. It's my first important job. And the last thing I need is to baby-sit you. Now, no more long-distance calls!"

"Okay, like, I wasn't born yesterday, Paul," said Molly, not moving from the chair. "Like, I was *not* making any long-distance calls. I've got some extra billys—you know, from working at the store—and I was, like, calling Tiffany. We were going to go to Lakedale. I need some, like, mascara, fer sure."

Hawkeye, Amy, and Justin, their conversation drowned out by the argument, couldn't help but notice what was going on.

"They got into a fight the last time I was here, too," said Amy quickly, rolling her green eyes. "And my pizza was burned to a crisp. For the sake of my stomach, I'm going to be the umpire for this one."

Amy took a deep breath and walked up to the phone.

"What's the matter?" she asked.

Paul said, "My parents just got hooked up to one of those new long-distance phone services. You know, you call up the computer from anywhere in town, give the access number, and then make your call. Well, ever since then, Molly's been going to phone booths all over town and making long-distance phone calls."

"Like, I totally stopped," said Molly in a huffy voice. "Dad, like, came up to me and said it just wasn't cool, so I just, you know, stopped."

Paul hit the phone with his fist. "Molly, when are you going to quit that Valley Girl talk of yours? You know, it's really out of date. People just don't talk like that any more. Hey, I bet you were talking with those friends of yours in California. I bet *that's* who you called on the phone service!"

Molly shook her head. "Hey, you're, like, making fun of the way I talk! I talk this way because—because, like, it's, you know, me. It's just the way I talk."

In the kitchen, a loud buzzer went off. Paul was so upset, though, that he didn't budge.

"Paul!" said Amy, nudging him. "Our pizza's going to burn. Then it'll be another twenty years before we get another one."

Paul began to move away. "Yeah, all right. I'll go get it. But you make sure she doesn't make another call."

"Like, I'm sure I'm going to!" Molly said sarcastically.

Paul groaned and hurried into the kitchen. "I can't believe I'm related to her!"

"Hey," shouted Amy after Paul. "Think I can prove whether she was calling or not?"

"Pizza's on me if you can!" he hollered, disappearing into the kitchen.

"Free pizza—all right!" Amy licked her lips in anticipation.

Molly rolled her eyes in disbelief. "You mean, you can, like, prove whether or not I was, like, calling California?"

"Sure," said Amy as she turned toward her table. "I think this one's going to be simple. I'll get Hawkeye to do one of his drawings, and that'll *show* which one of you is right."

Amy hurried back to her table.

"Paul'll give us free pizza if we can prove whether or not Molly was calling long distance," she said excitedly. "I know who's right, but can you do a drawing to show them, Hawkeye?"

Amy Adams   **Hawkeye Collins**

Young Sleuths Detect Fun in Mysteries

By Alice Cory
Staff Writer

Lakewood Hills has two new super sleuths watching over its citizens. They are Christopher "Hawkeye" Collins and Amy Amanda Adams, both 12 years old and sixth-grade students at Lakewood Hills Elementary.

Christopher Collins, the popular, blond, blue-eyed sleuth

of 128 Crestview Drive, is better known by his nickname, "Hawkeye." His father, Peter Collins, who is an attorney downtown, explains, "We started calling him Hawkeye many years ago because he notices everything, even tiny details. That's what makes him so good at solving mysteries." His mother, Linda Collins, a real estate agent, agrees: "Yes, but he

Sleuths continued on page 4A

CONTENTS

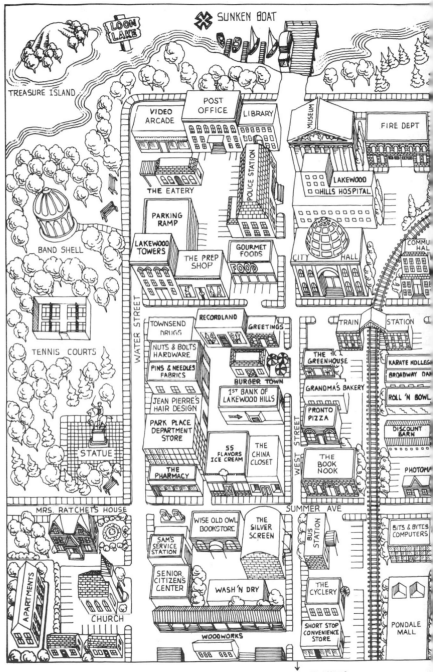

Sleuths continued from page 2A

also started to draw at a very early age. His sketches capture everything he sees. He draws clues or the scene of the crime — or anything else that will help solve a mystery."

Amy Adams, a spitfire with red hair and sparkling green eyes, lives right across the street, at 131 Crestview Drive. Known to many as the star of the track team, she is also a star math student. "She's quick of mind, quick of foot and quick of temper," says her teacher, Ted Bronson, chuckling. "And she's never intimidated." Not only do she and Hawkeye share the same birthday, but also the same love of mysteries.

"If something's wrong," says Amy, leaning on her ten-speed, "you just can't look the other way."

"Right," says Hawkeye, pulling his ever-present sketch pad and pencil from his back pocket. "And if we can't solve a case right away, I'll do a drawing of the scene of the crime. When we study my sketch, we can usually figure out what happened."

When the two detectives are not playing video games or soccer (Hawkeye is the captain of the sixth-grade team), they can often be seen biking around town, making sure justice is done. Occa-

sionally aided by Hawkeye's frisky golden retriever, Nosey, and Amy's six-year-old sister, Lucy, they've solved every case they've handled to date.

How did the two get started in the detective business?

It all started last year at Lakewood Hills Elementary's Career Days. There the two met Sergeant Treadwell, one of Lakewood Hills' best-known policemen. Of Hawkeye and Amy, Sergeant Treadwell proudly brags, "They're terrific. Right after we met, one of the teachers had a whole pile of tests stolen. I sure couldn't figure out who had done it, but Hawkeye did one of his sketches and he and Amy had the case solved in five minutes! You can't fool those two."

Sergeant Treadwell adds: "I don't know what Lakewood Hills ever did without Hawkeye and Amy. They've found a dognapped dog, located stolen video games, and cracked many other tough cases. Why, whenever I have a problem I can't solve, I know just where to go — straight to those two super sleuths!"

> **" They've found a dognapped dog, located stolen video games, and cracked many other tough cases. "**

Ends Today!

SAL

"You mean you can, like, prove whether or not I was calling California?" Molly said.

"I'm not that good on an empty stomach," he said, reaching into his back pocket, "but for free pizza—I'll give it my best shot!"

Hawkeye pulled out his sketch pad and pencil and followed Amy back to the phone. They looked over the phone, and then Hawkeye began to draw everything he saw. Molly just sat there in the chair, a bored, disgusted look on her face.

Hawkeye finished his drawing a couple of minutes later, just as Paul came out of the kitchen, a steaming pizza in his hand.

"Well," he said, "did she or didn't she?"

"See for yourself," said Amy, handing Hawkeye's sketch to Paul.

DID MOLLY CALL LONG DISTANCE OR DIDN'T SHE?

S O L U T I O N

See page 81

The Mystery of Lucy's Disappearance

"She's been missing for five hours!" Amy told Hawkeye as she opened the door to let him in. "She's with the twins—they're all missing."

It was almost her bedtime, and Lucy still wasn't home. The sun had set hours ago, it was windy and pitch black outside, and thunder clouds were approaching.

Hawkeye stepped into Amy's house. "No one has any idea where they are?"

"Nope. And Mom and Dad are going nuts, too. Dad's calling the police right now." Amy sighed. "I hope she's okay."

Hawkeye's eyes started searching the room. He glanced over at the table in the family room, then scanned the kitchen counter.

Amy knew what he was doing. "I already looked for clues. I couldn't find anything."

Hawkeye frowned. "Didn't Lucy say anything about where she was going?" he asked.

"I know she was going to play with the twins this afternoon, but she didn't say where. The big rule is that we're always supposed to tell someone where we're going—but this time she didn't. We're never supposed to leave the house without—"

Suddenly, Amy's father called out. "Amy, come here!"

Her mother added, "We've found something!"

Hawkeye and Amy hurried into the kitchen. They found Mr. and Mrs. Adams staring at a piece of paper.

"We were just about to dial the police," said Mrs. Adams, "when we found this on the floor."

Mr. Adams stepped aside so that Amy and Hawkeye could see.

"It must have fallen off the message board. This is Lucy's handwriting, all right—but what does it say? Can you two make any sense of this?"

Amy and Hawkeye read the note. Amy couldn't make any sense of it, but she knew right away what it was.

"It's a code!" she exclaimed. "It's another one of Lucy's codes!"

"Hey," said Hawkeye, "I'll bet it tells where

she went. She never says anything straight if she can use a code."

"Well, I have a feeling she's in trouble, so let's hope we can break the darn thing!" said Mr. Adams.

Mrs. Adams was totally confused by the code. "What on earth can it mean?"

"Look at all the names of animals," said Hawkeye.

Mr. Adams said, "Maybe I should call the zoo."

"This is no time for jokes," said Mrs. Adams sharply.

Amy studied the message a moment, squinting as her eyes scanned the words. "Hey," she muttered, "I think I see something."

Hawkeye pulled his sketch pad and pencil out of his back pocket and handed them to Amy.

"Here, Amy," he said. "Work it out on paper. That always helps me."

"Good idea," Amy agreed.

She took the paper and started to copy the list from the coded message Lucy had left on the board.

"You're always supposed to look for the common or repeating things in codes," said Amy as she wrote.

No sooner had she copied the last word than she realized something.

"I've got it!" Amy said. "I know where Lucy and the twins are."

"I've got it!" she said. "I know where Lucy and the twins are. And we'd better move fast, because I bet they're in trouble!"

WHERE WERE LUCY AND THE TWINS?

See page 83

The Secret of the Software Spy

Sergeant Treadwell peered out the restaurant window and looked at the outdoor eating area.

"One of those people is an international computer spy known as Jean LeMal, and I really need your help to catch him," said the sergeant to Hawkeye, Amy, and Mrs. von Buttermore. "Can I count on you?"

Hawkeye and Amy nodded eagerly. "You're on," they said.

Mrs. von Buttermore smiled. "You can always count on a von Buttermore, Sergeant."

"Good. I knew you'd help," said Sergeant Treadwell. "He's already stolen software, including some really valuable programs, from three computer companies here in town. You remember, Hawkeye and Amy, you went over to the Computer Data company with me to investigate one of those robberies. Anyway, everyone's certain that this spy plans to sell the software on the international market."

"I bet he'll sell them for big bucks, too," said Hawkeye.

"But how do you know he's here, Sarge?" asked Amy.

Sergeant Treadwell smiled proudly. "Well, I received a tip about an hour ago that he'd be at this restaurant making contact with another spy."

The sergeant held back the curtain so that they could all see out. It was lunchtime at the outdoor cafe, and almost all the tables were full.

"Goodness!" exclaimed Mrs. von Buttermore. "I think this is all rather exciting. It's like one of those old movies where the case is solved by a dashing detective."

"Well, thank you, Mrs. von Buttermore," said Sergeant Treadwell, going a little red in the face.

Mrs. von Buttermore smiled. "What should we look for, Sergeant?"

"We don't know too much." Sergeant Treadwell opened his note pad. "So just look for suspicious behavior. This man—the spy—is French, but he doesn't have an accent. He's very sophisticated and smart."

"Sophisticated and smart," repeated Mrs. von Buttermore, brushing a wisp of grey hair back from her face. "Don't worry—I can spot that type a mile away. Come on, let's go. I'm starved."

"Good," said Sergeant Treadwell. "You three go on. I'll be out as soon as I change into my disguise."

"What's it going to be this time, Sarge?" asked Amy, fearing the worst. "I hope not another little old lady."

"No, that disguise doesn't seem to work very well on me." The sergeant patted his belly and laughed. "This time I'm going to be a waiter."

Hawkeye elbowed Amy and, under his breath, muttered, "Uh-oh, very dashing!"

Hawkeye and Amy followed Mrs. von Buttermore to the door that led out onto the patio. They were greeted by a Frenchman in a tuxedo.

"*Bonjour,* Pierre," she said, adjusting her diamond bracelet. "A table for three."

The head waiter clicked his heels. "Immediately, madame."

He gave them the finest table available, one with a bright red-and-yellow umbrella to protect them from the strong sunshine. But they hardly noticed where they were sitting. They were too busy searching the place with their eyes.

"Boy," said Hawkeye, his eyes everywhere, "it's hard to imagine that one of these people is a spy."

"Shh, Hawkeye!" whispered Amy. "Not so loud!"

Mrs. von Buttermore glanced about, as if she were quite naturally admiring the people in the restaurant. "Still, it is rather hard to imagine there's a spy here," she commented.

Amy glanced to the side and did a double take. "Oh, brother. Don't look now, but guess who's coming."

Sergeant Treadwell came out, wearing a black vest that didn't quite make it all the way around his stomach, and a bow tie that drooped. Balanced precariously on one shoulder was a tray heaped with food.

"Oh, I hope—I hope he—" began Hawkeye.

Suddenly, there was an enormous crash. Everyone turned to see what had happened.

"Oh, dear," said Mrs. von Buttermore. "An entire tray of food."

Hawkeye buried his face in his hands. "Sarge is a walking disaster area," he said, under his breath. "They should issue safety warnings when he's around."

Sergeant Treadwell had tripped and dumped six plates of food on one of the customers. The outraged woman was now dripping in tender cuts of beef, slices of fresh vegetables, and delicate French sauces.

"Oh, I'm sorry!" said Sergeant Treadwell, trying to brush the woman off. "I'm so, so sorry!"

The woman picked up a piece of meat from her plate and threw it at him.

"You fool!" she cried. "Get away!"

"But, but—" pleaded Sergeant Treadwell.

The head waiter, his face red, scurried over and grabbed the sergeant by the arm. In a thick French accent, he shouted, "You are fired! Now, get out!"

"Boy," said Hawkeye, "that was the shortest career I've ever seen."

"Really," said Amy, grinning. "You know, Sarge never has much luck with his disguises."

Mrs. von Buttermore unfolded her napkin. "Well, my dears, looks like we're on our own. It's up to us to spot this spy."

Hawkeye glanced at Amy. "I think—"

Amy nodded and finished his sentence. "—we can handle it."

Hawkeye pulled out his sketch pad and opened it to a fresh page. He glanced around and started drawing. Maybe, just maybe, he could spot something.

"Let me know if you see anything suspicious," he told Mrs. von Buttermore and Amy.

Amy gasped. "I do. That man over there with the moustache."

The man turned around slightly and Mrs. von Buttermore got a better view of his face.

"Oh, him?" murmured Mrs. von Buttermore. "That's Monsieur Tortue—the owner of the restaurant."

"Drats," said Amy. "I just noticed that he was eating a little differently."

"There's one man here who sure looks like a good suspect!" said Hawkeye.

Mrs. von Buttermore nodded. "That's the French way."

Hawkeye continued with his sketch. He drew in Monsieur Tortue and his table, and got in a few more tables nearby. As he was drawing one of the people, however, he began to notice something. He finished his sketch, then examined it.

"Hey, I don't know if this is the real spy," Hawkeye said, pointing to the drawing, "but there's one man here who sure looks like he's a good suspect!"

WHICH MAN DID HAWKEYE SUSPECT WAS THE INTERNATIONAL SPY?

See page 85

The Case of the Book Lover's Treasure Hunt

There were only two clues left to go in the annual Book Lover's Treasure Hunt, and Hawkeye and Amy were in the lead. With any luck, they were certain to win the prize—a certificate for ten books of their choice.

"Okay, now we're supposed to find out where Sherlock Holmes lived," said Hawkeye, poring over a book.

"Yeah, and that should tell us where to go next," said Amy, twiddling a piece of her red hair as she flipped through a book. "We're sure getting close. If only we can just find this last riddle."

Hawkeye jumped right out of his chair, his fists raised in victory. "Allll *right*! Here it is, the last riddle, stuck in this chapter called 'The Baker Street Sleuth!' " He lifted a piece of paper out of the book.

"Here, let me read it, too," said Amy, snatching it from him in excitement.

She unfolded it and held it out for them both to see.

"Hey, this is a hard one," she said. "Look, it's a two-part riddle."

"Okay, let's do the first part," said Hawkeye.

PART I: WHERE YOU GO NEXT

There have been many places in history
Where detectives could crack a good
    mystery,
But a great place to find 'em
Is after they bind 'em,
Where the clerks know the wares and
    can scurry.

"So this one tells us where to go next." Amy's green eyes sparkled with excitement as she studied it. " 'After they bind 'em'— hey, they must be talking about books again."

"Yeah." Hawkeye nodded as he continued reading. " 'Where the clerks know the wares'— sounds like a store, not a library."

Hawkeye and Amy looked at one another and at the same instant, both said, "The Book Nook—it's got to be the bookstore!"

Hawkeye added, pointing to the first two lines of the riddle, "I bet it's in the mystery section."

"You bet. That's where detectives like us crack mysteries—and crack open mystery books! Let's go for it!" Amy replied.

They jumped to their feet and began stashing the books back on the shelves.

"A piece of cake!" exclaimed Hawkeye.

"Yeah," said Amy, grinning, "but we've got to get there before anybody else."

Hawkeye looked at Amy and pointed to the piece of paper. "What are we waiting for?"

"Right!" said Amy with a big grin. "And now, off to the bookstore for the final clue—and victory!"

Hawkeye and Amy raced out of the library.

"Come on, Nosey, let's go!" said Hawkeye, untying his dog, who had been waiting outside for them.

The three of them charged off, and it was only a matter of moments before Hawkeye and Amy reached the Book Nook.

"Hang on a sec. I've got to park Nosey over here." He scrambled over to a parking meter and attached Nosey's leash to it. "I'll be right back, Nosey."

He started away, thought better of it, then turned and reached into his pocket. He quickly took out a dime and put it in the parking meter.

Seeing this, Amy said, "What do you think they're going to do? Give her a ticket?"

Hawkeye shrugged and jogged up to her. "No, I just didn't want her to get towed."

"Oh, brother," said Amy in disbelief.

They walked into the bookstore as casually as possible and made their way through the customers browsing by the book racks. When they finally arrived at the mystery section, they took out the riddle and read the second part.

PART II: WHERE THE PRIZE IS HIDDEN AT THAT LOCATION

There once was a thing that was not;
It came and went on the dot.
The parents were shaken,
But no kids were taken,
And the crook was booked on the spot.

"I have a feeling the rest of this is *not* going to be a piece of cake," whispered Amy. "Here, hand me the riddle. I'll study it while—"

"Yeah, yeah, yeah," said Hawkeye, cutting her off. "While I do a drawing. You know, one of these days you have to learn how to draw. I mean, I always do the drawing."

He pulled out his sketch pad and, hoping to find something, did a drawing of the bookshelf. Minutes later, he still hadn't come up with anything definite. He went over to Amy.

They turned to the bookshelf, ready to grab the book that held the hidden prize.

"There's a lot of stuff here," he said, discouraged. "Did you come up with anything?"

Amy shrugged. "Not really. Here, listen while I read the second riddle again."

Amy read through it. When she was finished, they looked at one another, puzzled. Then, without saying anything, they checked Hawkeye's drawing one more time.

"I think—I think—" began Hawkeye.

"I think we did it, too!" exclaimed Amy.

They turned to the bookshelf, ready to grab the book that held the hidden prize.

WHICH BOOK HAD THE PRIZE INSIDE IT?

See page 87

THE CASE OF THE VANISHING PRINCE

THE DESERTED HOUSE
PART 4

What Happened in Volumes 5, 6, and 7

To thank Hawkeye and Amy for recovering her grandfather's stolen Egyptian treasure, Mrs. von Buttermore invited them to Florida's fabulous amusement park, FunWorld. It was there that Hawkeye and Amy met Umberto.

The two sleuths later learned that Umberto was the Crown Prince of Madagala. While he was on one of the FunWorld rides with them, he was kidnapped by two thugs who were after the crown jewels of Madagala.

Aided by Umberto's bodyguards, Hawkeye and Amy chased the kidnappers through the Haunted Kingdom and into the Looking Glass Maze. In part three of this four-part adventure, the kidnappers had just escaped in a car, taking Umberto with them. The only clue that Hawkeye and Amy had was a torn map.

"This map tells us exactly where the kidnappers are taking Umberto!" Amy said.

The Deserted House

"What do you mean, you know where they took him?" Hawkeye asked Amy. "I mean, how do you know?"

"Look at the map," said Amy. "It's not just an ordinary map—it's got a secret code telling the kidnappers where to take Umberto."

"So there's someone else involved?"

Amy shrugged and was about to speak, when Mario, the moustached bodyguard, cut her off.

"Where did they take him?" he asked, pushing forward. "We have a car. We can follow them."

"Look at this map," said Amy. "There are letters missing from the alphabet at the top, and a number missing from the side. The missing letters at the top spell 'lot.' The missing number on the side is four. That's where they've taken Umberto—lot number four."

"And lot four is shown on the map. All right, Amy!" said Hawkeye, impressed. "There must be a house or something there, and that's where they've taken Umberto!"

"Good work, kids," said Geno, the heavyset bodyguard, stalking over and snatching the map from Amy. "We'll see you later."

"Hey, no dice!" said Amy, yanking the map back. "We're coming, too!"

"Yeah, it was our case first," added Hawkeye.

The bodyguards glanced at one another, whispered, and then shrugged.

"Okay," said Mario. "As we say in Madagala, four heads are better than one."

"Well," began Hawkeye, "in Lakewood Hills there's always a mystery, and *we* say, 'Eight feet are better than two.' "

"Oh brother," said Amy, wrinkling her nose impatiently. "Let's go!" She took off at a run, heading for the FunWorld parking lot.

Right behind her, Hawkeye and the bodyguards hurried through FunWorld toward the Magic Gates. Cutting through swarms of people, the bodyguards led the way to a long black car parked in front of the hotel. They jumped in, and Mario started the engine with a roar. He punched the gas pedal, the car lurched forward, and Hawkeye and Amy were thrown against the back seat.

"This isn't the kind of ride I expected at FunWorld," commented Hawkeye, trying to regain his balance.

"Really," agreed Amy. "I didn't see anything about this in the brochure."

They sped out of the parking lot and, following the map, drove along the ocean for ten miles before turning inland. There, the smooth, paved road quickly faded into Alligator Alley, an old dirt road built across the seemingly endless swamp.

"Hurry up, guys," said Hawkeye. "We've got to get there before they take Umberto away in a helicopter or something."

"Yeah, but watch it," said Amy, pointing to the road. "There's an alligator!"

Bouncing over deep potholes, they passed several deserted houses. About a mile later, they came to an island that rose out of the swamplands. Through the thick trees, they could just barely make out the top of an old chimney.

"This is lot number four," said Hawkeye. "And I'll bet the kidnappers have Umberto in that old house up there."

They all fell silent as Mario drove carefully onto the island and pulled to a stop behind a mass of overgrown bushes. Ahead of them was a small wooden house that was in ruins. From where they were, they could see no movement in either the front two windows or the three side windows. Hawkeye and Amy leaned forward in their seats.

"It sure looks empty to me," said Amy. "There's no car or anything." She pointed to the road, which curved back into the swamp. "I hope they didn't just stop here and go on."

Hawkeye studied the road. "Look at those car tracks up there. They look pretty fresh."

"Let's go take a look," whispered Geno, getting out. "But we have to be very quiet."

"Right," said Hawkeye. "If the kidnappers *are* here, I don't think they're going to like a surprise visit."

Amy nodded. "For sure."

They eased their way out of the car one at a time, carefully shutting the doors behind them. They paused for a moment, listening. There wasn't a sound. Then, their bodies tense and their eyes wide, they made their way up to the old house.

As they neared the house, Mario whispered, "It looks deserted."

Geno shook his head. "You never know."

Hawkeye and Amy inched their way onto the front porch. They heard a sound and froze. Silence. Hawkeye cautiously reached for the screen door and whispered, "This is pretty—"

Suddenly they heard a scream from just inside the door. At the same moment, a dark object fell on Hawkeye and Amy, trapping them. They screamed and fought frantically to get loose.

"Hey, wait," said Amy after a few seconds. "It's just the screen door."

Hawkeye stopped punching the air and stood still. The large screen door, thick with grime, had loosened from its hinges and fallen on them. The screen itself had ripped and folded around them as it fell, trapping them like fish in a net.

"Fooled me," said Hawkeye, turning a little red with embarrassment. He grinned with relief, and then began to free himself from the screen. "I thought the kidnappers had us for sure."

Amy brushed herself off and pulled the torn screen away. "Well, no point in tiptoeing around anymore," she said. "If the kidnappers are here, they know all about us by now."

Hawkeye stepped into the house. "This place sure looks empty," he said. "It doesn't look like anyone's been here for months."

"Gee, and I was so sure about that clue—" Amy said. Her voice trailed off as she looked around the room.

Suddenly Hawkeye spotted something ragged hanging from the door frame. He reached for it.

"Hey, someone *has* been here," he said, holding up a ripped piece of cloth. "It looks like somebody's shirt or pants got snagged."

Mario bounded up the steps. "That's—that's a piece of Umberto's shirt." He cupped his hands around his mouth and shouted as loudly as he could, "Umberto! Umberto! Where are you?"

There was no response from the deserted house or from the jungle-like swamps and trees around it.

"Well," said Amy, "there've got to be some clues here. How about if you guys check outside, and we'll look around in here."

As the bodyguards searched around the outside of the house, Hawkeye and Amy went through every room. But they found nothing.

Amy shook her head. "I sure don't see anything. Poor Umberto. Maybe they *did* fly him out in a helicopter."

Hawkeye groaned. "I hope not. That'd mean we'd never be able to catch up with them." He paused, then pulled his sketch pad and pencil from his back pocket. "There's just something here that I don't get, Amy."

As he always did when a case didn't make sense, Hawkeye began to draw the scene around him.

"I know there's a clue here somewhere," he murmured to himself.

Five minutes later, Hawkeye had completed a floor plan of the house. He sat down in a wobbly old rocking chair and studied his sketch.

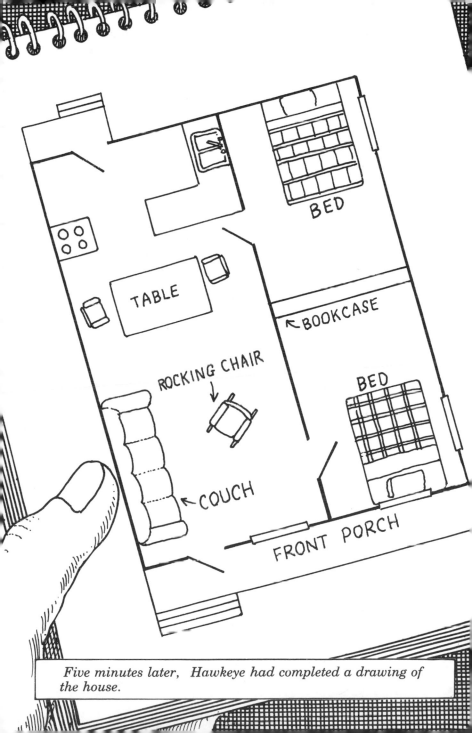

Five minutes later, Hawkeye had completed a drawing of the house.

"Somewhere," he muttered. "There's something wrong here somewhere. If only—"

The two bodyguards, looking disappointed, came into the house.

"Nothing!" said Geno in disgust.

Pulling on his moustache, Mario said, "We've lost them for sure now!"

"You can't give up so easily," Amy began. "I mean—"

Leaping out of the rocking chair, Hawkeye cut her off. "Amy's right. It's too early to give up—too early because I know where to find Umberto!"

WHERE WAS UMBERTO?

SOLUTION
See page 89

SOLUTIONS

The Mystery of the Missing Turkey

"Nosey didn't steal your turkey," Hawkeye told Mrs. Ratchet, "because those teeth marks on the roasting pan aren't hers."

Amy said, "Hawkeye, you're right. Look at Nosey's teeth marks in the frisbee. They're a lot bigger than the ones left on the roasting pan."

Mrs. Ratchet was forced to admit that Nosey hadn't stolen her turkey, after all. With Nosey's help, however, they did discover who the thieves were.

Following the smell of the turkey, Nosey led Hawkeye, Amy, and Mrs. Ratchet to a nearby tree. When they looked up into the branches, they saw three raccoons just finishing the last of the turkey.

"Oh, well," Mrs. Ratchet sighed. "Instead of a turkey, I guess I'll have a grilled peanut-butter sandwich."

Hawkeye and Amy exchanged glances.

"How about coming to my house for dinner?" Hawkeye asked.

Amy nodded. "Yeah, our families are

continued

having dinner together, and I'm sure there's plenty of food."

"Well," said Mrs. Ratchet, "I don't know. I'm not sure I want to eat with all those people."

"Oh, come on," said Hawkeye. "Don't be shy. I know everyone will like it if you eat with us."

"Really?" said Mrs. Ratchet, smiling for the first time in weeks. "Maybe I will, then. Well, thank you!"

The Case of the Tinsel-Teeth Teaser

The girl who wrote the letter was the one in the striped sweater.

"The handwriting was done by a left-handed person," said Hawkeye. "And there's only one girl in the group who doesn't write with her right hand."

"That's Jean!" exclaimed Joanna, just as classes were letting out and pouring into the hall. "Oh, Hawkeye, you're so smart!"

She gave him a big hug right in front of everyone.

His face burning red, Hawkeye said, "It's no big deal!"

The next day, when Joanna went to ask Jean about the note, Jean burst into tears.

"I'm sorry, Joanna, I didn't mean to hurt your feelings that much. And I went to the orthodontist yesterday afternoon—and found out I have to have braces, too!" she wailed.

The Case of the China Catastrophe

Amy, Hawkeye, and Sarge started looking for the culprit on the girl's basketball team.

"This sweater doesn't belong to one of the boys on the basketball team," exclaimed Amy. "It belongs to one of the girls—the one with the red hair!"

Amy quickly pointed out that the sweater belonged to a girl because it buttoned right over left.

"Good work!" said Hawkeye. He looked at his own shirt. "You're right, mine buttons left over right."

An hour later Sergeant Treadwell questioned Laurie, the only red-haired girl on the basketball team. She confessed to causing the damage.

"But I didn't do it on purpose, honest!" she pleaded. "I went in there looking for a Mother's Day present for my mom. Right after I got in the door, I tripped over a box. Then I fell against that big shelf and it tipped over. I was so scared that I just ran."

continued

When he heard the story, Mr. Norton apologized.

"Actually, I guess it's all my fault," he said. "I should know better than to leave packing boxes lying around in the store. I suppose it's lucky that nothing happened to Laurie, too!"

"With the case solved, Sergeant Tread-well quickly led Hawkeye and Amy back to the police station and their hot fudge sun-daes.

"And here's some extra colored sprin-kles for your good work!" he said.

To Amy, Hawkeye whispered, "I was kind of hoping we'd at least get another sun-dae!"

77

The Secret of the Mysterious Letters

"The woman who stole your briefcase," said Hawkeye to the grey-haired woman, "is named Mary Mathews. The letter to her is the only one that's been cancelled."

Hawkeye showed her the three envelopes.

"Of course," said Amy. "That letter is the only one that's been through the mail. The other two are all ready to be mailed—look, they've got stamps on them and everything. Mary Mathews must have received one letter and was about to mail the other two."

Hawkeye and Amy escorted the woman to the police station and explained what had happened. The police, who were very impressed, set off at once to find Mary Mathews.

Hawkeye and Amy then hurried off to the baseball game. The grey-haired woman, whose name was Elizabeth Peterson, decided to join them.

"I can't do any work this afternoon until the police recover the briefcase," she said, "so I might as well have some fun! And Hawkeye and Amy, the hot dogs and pop are on me."

79

The Mystery of Molly's Phone Call

Molly did not call long distance.

"At least, not on your parents' long-distance phone service," said Amy. She turned to Paul and continued, "She couldn't have, because the phone service uses a computer. And to communicate with a computer, you have to have a push-button phone!"

"Of course", said Hawkeye. "And this is a dial phone".

Paul realized his error. After reluctantly giving Hawkeye, Amy, and Justin their free pizza, he even more reluctantly apologized to his sister.

"I'm sorry, really I am," he said.

"Like, that's okay, Paul, totally", Molly replied as she stood up. "But I gotta go, 'cause they've got this mascara on saletoday only".

Paul grinned. "Well, then, like, go for it!".

READ THE SOLUTIONS IN YOUR MIRROR

The Mystery of Lucy's Disappearance

"The code says, 'Went to canoe on lake.' That's where Lucy and the twins are, canoeing on the lake," said Amy. "Look at all the names of animals here—every word after them is part of the coded message."

"Amy, you're right," said Hawkeye. "But we'd better hurry up and find them before that storm comes."

Wasting no time, Mr. and Mrs. Adams telephoned Sergeant Treadwell. A search party was formed, and Lucy and the twins were found, stranded on Treasure Island in the middle of Loon Lake. Breaking a strict rule, they had taken a canoe out on the lake and tried to reach the island. The canoe had tipped over but, luckily, Lucy, Buffy, and Duffy had been able to wade to the island.

As punishment for disobeying the rule, all three children were grounded for a month.

The Secret of the Software Spy

"The best suspect I've found so far," said Hawkeye, "is the man at the farthest table back, who's eating like a European. He has his fork in his left hand and his knife in his right hand—just like the owner of the restaurant!"

Together, Hawkeye and Amy wandered over near the man's table. As they slowly walked by, they overheard the suspicious man and another man talking about some super new software.

When she and Hawkeye were out of sight, Amy said, "That's him, all right."

She hurried out of the restaurant and gave a description of the man to Sergeant Treadwell, who was waiting in his squad car in the parking lot. He radioed for help, and moments later, several other policemen arrived.

Thanks to Hawkeye's and Amy's detective work, Sergeant Treadwell and the other policemen successfully captured the international computer spy.

SOLUTION

READ THE SOLUTIONS IN YOUR MIRROR

The Case of the Book Lover's Treasure Hunt

The book with the prize inside was The Vanishing School Bus.

"Something that vanishes," said Amy, "could be something that vanished."

"Right," said Hawkeye. "And a school bus comes and goes right on time—you know, right on the job."

Hawkeye and Amy opened the book, which told the story of a school bus that disappeared, and found the winning prize certificate inside. They hurried up and showed it to the owner of the bookstore.

"You two are the winners, all right," said the bookseller. "Mrs. Buttermore sponsored the treasure hunt, and I know she'll be very pleased that you two are the winners. As a matter of fact, I think she was expecting you to win."

"Vanishing" was all Hawkeye and Amy could say when the bookstore owner told them they could each have their pick of ten books in the store.

continued

The Deserted House

"Umberto is hidden in a secret room, right in this house!" exclaimed Hawkeye.

Pointing to his drawing, he added, "Look. From the outside, there are three windows—but in my drawing, there are only two!"

"Omigosh," gasped Amy. "You're right, Hawkeye. And that must mean there's a secret room behind the bookshelves!"

With the help of the two bodyguards, Hawkeye and Amy quickly searched the room. They found a secret latch, turned it, and the bookshelves pulled open. There, in the secret room, was Umberto, a piece of cloth tied over his mouth so that he couldn't call out for help. Hawkeye and Amy quickly untied him.

"They're after the crown jewels!" exclaimed the Crown Prince. "Magdalena and I heard them say they were going back to the exhibit at the hotel to look at them one more time,"

They wasted no time in running back to the hotel. When he searched the crowd of people at the exhibit, Umberto recognized the

kidnappers, who were disguised as two old men. The bodyguards and police quickly arrested them and their accomplices, who had drawn the map.

That night, Mrs. von Buttermore, the King of Madagala, Umberto, the bodyguards, and Hawkeye and Amy all got together for a princely dinner—FunWorld's best hot dogs and french fries, washed down with chocolate malts.

Prince Umberto and his father, the King of Madagala, invited Hawkeye and Amy to visit Madagala soon. Mrs. von Buttermore promised Hawkeye and Amy that she would take them there next year.